The Tide

Chapter 1

Wake up, get dressed, go eat, get coffee, go to school, zone out, come home, go on the computer until three in the morning filling the emptiness in my heart onto the depths of the internet, then repeat the process.

Life has a plethora of incredibly painful moments, all with the drug like highs of good moments in between the shitty ones. However, those highs don't come easy for some, and when I finally got my high it all came crashing and burning. Maybe it was for the best. My name is Finn Mackay and this is my story.

One morning in December, I woke to the ear piercing sound of my alarm clock ringing like a bomb about to explode right there on my night stand. Not realizing how late I actually was, I hit snooze and went back to bed. I waited for my father to walk in and yell at me to "get the hell up and stop being a lazy piece of shit", yet no one came to my room.

Dad didn't come to come yell at me, no mom to warn me that dad was about to kill me, or no sister to come and tell me I'm a crappy older brother for doing something I probably don't know or care about. It was different. I waited for what seemed like a long time. I looked at my phone hoping that it was 5:00 A.M. and my alarm clock just went crazy for some reason. I hit the power button and waited for the stupid piece of shit to turn on. I went to grab my phone and looked at it like I was confronted by the cops after drinking. Before my mind could even comprehend what was happening, I jumped out of bed and dashed to my desk checking what day it was on the calendar.

"Oh shit…"

It was Friday. My parents leave for work early on Friday, how could I forget this important thing that seems to happen every single week? Then the worst part hit me…

"Current event." I had one of the biggest grades of the year due today, and I slept in. Wearing nothing more than jogger pants and a Red Hot Chili Peppers shirt with the sleeves cut off that I wore to bed, I grabbed my backpack with my unfinished homework in it. I ran out of the house faster than Usain Bolt on steroids and ran around to the side of the house to grab my bike. I raced for the school a little less than three miles down the road. What I did not notice on the door of my house that looked to be very reminiscent of a "1950s American Dream" was a note from my father that read:

"You're late." I thanked my dad for the lovely reminder of how much of a fuck-up I am.

I finally reached my high school and I whipped open the doors of the school and hit the buzzer that would intercom the front office to allow me inside. I checked my phone while I waited for a response. 9:40 A.M. it read. I have five minutes to get to class or I'm screwed.

"How may I help you?" the buzzer asked with the secretary's voice echoing around me.

"Student drop off," I answered.

"Come on in." A pause, then "click", the door was open.

I swung that door open like I owned the place. That's right, I'm here and there is no way in hell anything can stop me now. I entered the office and obtained the pink slip that said I was here today. I checked my phone. 9:43 A.M. I started to panic as I rushed to the stairs and flew up them like Superman, then around the last step it hit me, literally. I tripped and fell and saw everything around me blur. I slowly got up from the fall to see the feet of someone standing in front of me. As I got off the ground I realized who it was.

It was Kylynn Ross, the one girl I wished never saw that happen. She was a bit younger than me, but not by much. Kylynn made my soul melt, but then I realized something that was surprisingly more important than Kylynn. I got up and tried not to acknowledge my crush. I got to the room on the end of the wing, swung open the door, and handed Mr. Rider the pink paper along with my papers for the presentation. I was ready to start.

"You're late Finn." Mr. Rider spoke as his eyes glared "you goofed up" at me.

"What?" I asked as a rush of feelings enveloped me. I felt like murder was a good option, but then I thought to cry, yeah maybe crying was good.

"You're late, I'm sorry but you lost the chance to get it to me." The blood drained from my body leaving my face a pale canvas of shock.

"Are you kidding me? I worked my ass off to get here and you do this to me because I'm a minute late? One minute? What kind of teacher are you?" I roared at Mr. Rider, well at least I thought I did.

"Finn?...Finn?...Finn!" I snapped back to reality.

"What?"

"Did you hear me? You can get it to me tomorrow. Now take your seat now." Mr. Rider walked away as I trudged to my seat and leaned over to my table mate.

"What just happened?" I asked.

"You zoned out, Finn." My table mate responded.

"Oh," I spoke as I switched gears to work on my history paper about the French and Indian War or something like that.

Chapter 2

After a grueling 70 minutes of history class, even though I missed 20 minutes of it, I was just about ready to go back to that hobbit hole I call my bedroom. Back to my Twitter, back to my Tumblr, back to my YouTube, places where I can be myself. The only issue here is that school doesn't just go away until you graduate high school, you then make the easy choice to go to college and not have to live with your parents. I mean, it's not like I would be missed; I don't spend any time with them as it is. For the past five years ever since they got their new jobs, I have never even spent my birthday with them. They are always working and it's the one day of the year I actually want to spend time with my family and I can't. I mean, I'm not complaining. At least I have a family and I have people to give me some sort of gift each year, but even though I have this, it is still not perfect and never will be.

The bell rang for lunch. Finally, the time of the day where I can hang out with "friends" (although I'm still not being myself) and get teased by these so called "friends" because I'm nice to the not-so-popular kids. I don't get it. I'm respectful to everyone, I don't care who you are whether you're not exactly "in shape", or have some sort of difficulty. Then I also get teased for respecting the kids who are different from them. Now by "different" I don't mean not active or not sporty wise. I mean kids that are a different sexuality, ethnicity, or by their religious beliefs. I 100% respect people of different; religions, sexuality, race, or anything of that nature, and because of my kindness I am teased by my "friends". Funny thing is they honestly are not even my friends they are only nice to me one on one, when it's a group I am treated like shit.

I walk into lunch to sit down with these "friends", but they are not there. It took me some time to realize they were sitting in a new spot in the cafeteria. When I went over to sit down they sent me away because there were no more seats, clearly there were more seats. This happened to be the one time I actually wanted to sit with them. For as shy as I am, I'd like to think I am a relatively sarcastic person so I tried to use that to my advantage.

"Hey guys, how's it going?" They all looked at me with blank stares "Sounds like a great time, I'm just gonna slide right in if that is a-okay with you guys."

As I had reached for a seat next to the ringleader of the ass-hats someone stood up from the other side of the table. He walked over behind me, I slid the seat back and went to sit down. Andy, the kid who walked over behind me pulled the seat out. The weight of my backpack took me to the ground faster than I would have already. When I looked up Andy was standing over me.

"Nice to see you again Andrew. By any chance do you remember fourth grade? We were best friends; now how did we get here?" Andy looked at me like a kangaroo ready to quite literally kick the shit at me.

Before that could happen the lead ass-hat got up from his chair and helped me up. He was bigger than me, stronger too. Wasn't always like that, I remember he cried in 6th grade after I bumped into him in the hallway and he fell to the ground.

"Just go away Finn there's no more seats, right?" I stayed quiet, I broke eye contact and bent down to get my bag and walked away. I usually I go hide away in the library and forget to eat my lunch, looks like today is no different I suppose.

****

When I got home I went to my room and assumed the position I like to call the "physiological internet addiction position" and all it really looked like was me sitting in my computer chair slumped over and scrolling through whatever part of the internet I decide to drown myself in; It's a beautiful thing. After about an hour on the computer, I got a text from some number I did not know. It read:

"Hey I hope I have the right number, but this is Kylynn I saw you fall today. Sorry for laughing like I did, it was just kind of funny. I was hoping we could talk more?"

At that moment, my life felt complete. I was beyond happy. I can't tell you how fast I was texting. My mind was not even controlling my fingers anymore. As I was typing, I was convinced I was going to say

"Hey you're pretty, I'm in love with you, let's get married, have children, and live happy till we die." Lucky for me I simply just said:

"Hey, yeah this is Finn."

For the first time in what seemed like forever, I got out of my chair happy. I mean it was Friday I'm getting a hug from the girl I was crushing on this was possibly the best day of my life.

"Hey!" she replied back. The whole time as we were conversing I was shaking uncontrollably. I had trouble comprehending that I was actually talking to her. As we talked I fantasized that one day maybe we would sit in a field on a starry night, carve our names into a tree, telling the world we were in love. Maybe we would go on a journey across the world together. Over time my senses eased and I calmed down. Maybe we would grow old together, I doubt it she would just leave me when she realizes how much of a freak I am, everyone else thinks it, why would she not think so? No Finn stop thinking that way, things will work out.

"So, you saw me fall huh…"

19

"Yeah lol... I'm a klutz too, so it's okay." My hands began to stop shaking.

"You don't seem like one to be honest." Oh god am I flirting? I suck at flirting.

"Aw, thanks." Why no winking faces, I thought to myself. Winky faces are good, why are there none? The conversation went on for a little more time, but not very long, three or four minutes max. The conversation in complete honesty had nothing special about it, I was just drawn to her. Her personality bled through the phone and I loved it. She was just so outgoing and she just had something special about her.

She had asked me to meet her at school the following day.

I went up to the dirty blonde haired girl and gave her an awkward hug, but as we hugged our eyes locked. I looked at her in a way I never looked at anyone. We got close then while our faces were inches from each other we stopped. She backed away slightly.

"Well uh, I gotta go." She spoke. I nodded and waved to her as she began walked away, but then she stopped. "Maybe I'll go with you?" I nodded and we both walked to my locker together.

"So Finn are you going to the football game tonight?" She asked. Damn it,

I forgot about the game tonight, but I very rarely go to those kind of things anyways.

"Uh yeah, I just need a ride." I thought in my head that there was not a chance in hell she would be able to bring me.

"I can bring you if you want, I'm already bringing some of my other friends too. I'm sure we can fit you If you're cool with that?" Without even thinking I responded with a yes.

"Sounds like a plan, I'll see you at seven." She said with a sly smile.

Chapter 3

I was home alone again that night, convinced Kylynn would not show up. It was starting to get late, the game had already started. I slowly walked to my room in disappointment for actually thinking she would show up. I threw my phone on the ground. When it hit, the screen cracked just like my heart started to do. The impact triggered music to play, but I was fine with it. The Strokes started to play and I fell back on my bed. The clock read 7:30 P.M. she was 30 minutes late. I saw the headlights of a car pull into my driveway through my window. I walked down the stairs shocked to see Kylynn driving and her two friends sitting in the back of the 2005 Toyota Minivan. I ran out the door slamming it shut as I walked down the steps to the rocky driveway. Because I'm me, I forgot to lock the door so I walked back up the stairs, locked the door, and walked back down and saw all of the girls including Kylynn giggling. I opened the door and sat down for the two-minute car ride of awkwardness.

I had so many questions I could ask like: "Why so late?" or "What were you guys doing?" but I did not let it get to me. I just sat there in silence as we sat at the game and talked. I noticed little things I did not notice before. The way she laughed. It was subtle, yet constant. It was quiet but cute. She would occasionally laugh louder than usual. I'm not sure if it was on purpose or not, but I liked it. She always had a smile on her face. I never once saw her with a straight face. Her long dirty blonde hair sat below her shoulders. She had blue eyes that shined like the stars. I complimented her on her outfit, such a basic flirt. She smiled and became sort of shy. She explained how she thought it made her seem overweight. That made no sense to me on why she would say such a thing, she seemed as if she had so much confidence. Yet, she was not skinny, but she was not fat either. She was lean, built strong. She was tan, not super dark, but you could clearly tell that when winter came her skin would not be pale.

She often talked about bands she liked. Alternative and classic rock mostly; Twenty One Pilots, Hozier, The Beatles. After some time, she turned the conversation around on me and started complementing me on my clothes, how I looked, and stuff like that. As we talked back and forth she mentioned a song by Twenty One Pilots that I should listen to. It was Called "Ruby", she said it's an older one, but it is worth hearing. She complimented my hair and she liked that I had it gelled up, but if I was lazy I

26

could put it in a headband. She thought it was "hipster", whatever that means. She talked about how she liked the joggers I wore. She quickly pointed out that I would cross my one arm across my chest. She asked me why I do it, but I did not have a good answer.

"You're protecting something." I tilted my head.

"What do you mean?" I asked she thought for a moment

"The way you put your hand over your chest. There is clearly a reason. Is it fear? No, you're scared of your own mind. It gets the best of you and you clearly don't

know how to cope with it. I can help you."
She said with a smile.

After the game, we talked on the phone.
Kylynn told me that she liked me. She said
she was not fully ready to commit, but she
did have feelings and did not want her
concerns to get in the way.

"I don't know Finn." I was laying on
my floor with my phone on speaker in my
hand.

"Come on, why not?" I asked her,
my needy-ness very clearly was bleeding
through the phone. "What do we have to
lose?" There was silence for a moment. My
heart was pounding and my head was racing.

"Please?" I said, "Let's give it a chance." I could hear her footsteps as she paced back and forth on the hardwood floor in her room. The sound coming through the phone only made me more nervous. Then finally she spoke.

"You are right, fuck it."

Chapter 4

I had been coming out of my last block class and Kylynn had been walking by.

"Kylynn!" I shouted out at her, she had her headphones in and had not heard me. It wasn't the end of the world; it was a fairly normal thing she did. It's something you get used to. I made my way over to my locker and gathered my shit. My locker was fairly empty, nothing more than a few empty water bottles a sweatshirt that had been untouched for months and a book or two. In all honesty I don't even need anything from my locker, I just go to make it seem like I have something to do. I shut the door (I had to kick it a few times to fully close) and was on my way.

I made my way down Kylynn's hallway and leaned up against her set of lockers. She shut her door and there I was.

"Hey!" She said as she leaned in and kissed me. "What's going on?"

"Not too much, are we going to get food?" I asked. She rolled her eyes and pushed herself off of the lockers and made her way down the hallway. I followed a step or two behind.

"Why do we always have to get food?" She said clearly frustrated "We always go out and do stuff, why can't we just chill out for a little?" I didn't know how to respond.

"Whenever I wanna chill you always wanna go out." She stopped in her tracks then turned and gave me the, "Shut up and do what I say look". I didn't fight her, that's a battle I'd lose every time.

"Alright, lead the way" I responded. She gave me a very sassy smile and kept walking. We walked out of the school to the student parking lot. Most of the cars had already left, she was clearly frustrated due to the fact she prided herself on being the first one out of the school and home. It was probably my fault but I didn't say anything. I got into her car and reached for the AUX cord. The Growlers song "Black Memories" played.

"Kylynn, this is the song I wanted you to listen to! Did you check it out?" I asked her. She put her bag in the back and shut the truck.

"It's alright." She said as she got into the driver's seat. She threw the car in reverse and pulled out of the parking spot. "When are you gonna get your license? You should be driving me around."

"Eventually," I said unconvincingly.

"Yeah, sure." She said under her breath. We didn't exactly talk the car ride, she seemed in a pissy mood and I didn't wanna get her any more pissed than she was.

"You can just drop me off at home, I have a lot of shit to get done," I told her. She put up much less of a fight then I had thought she would.

"Alright, no problem." We pulled up to my house and let me out at the mailbox. I kissed her goodbye and made my way to the house. I opened the door like usual no one seemed to be home. I dropped my shit at the door and walked my ass up the stairs to my

room. My mom seemed to clean the house,
she always wanted to keep it in tip-top shape
for all of the visitors we didn't have coming.
My room however was shut to keep the
mess hidden. I opened the door and fell back
on my bed. Something seemed off about
Kylynn. She was always a little strange,
that's why I loved her.

Chapter 5

A Few Months later

"The End" by The Doors was playing in my room as her car rolled up, but I was half asleep. I had been working on a paper since the second I got home and redbull cans were spread across my room. She knocked on the door, but no one answered. She knocked again and my mom swung open the door. I could vaguely hear the conversation.

"Oh hi Kylynn, how are you?" Kylynn smiled at my mom.

"I'm good how are you, by any chance is Finn here?" My mom nodded, and let Kylynn in.

"I think he is working on a paper, but you can go up he probably needs the company." Kylynn smiled. She made her way up the steps. She opened my door slightly and peered in. I was at my desk turned away, I could relatively hear her but I payed little attention to it.

"Only a little longer than it's over." She told herself and walked in. She shut the door and went to my desk where a jar of money I had kept for a rainy day. She then moved to my bed and sat down.

"Hey silly, I'm here." I turned to see the most beautiful face in the world.

"Oh hey," I said and smiled at her. I got up and sat next to her, I leaned in and kissed her.

"What are you doing here?" I asked causing her to blush.

"Well I'm here to see you of course," She quickly responded. I laughed.

"I know that," I said. She smiled. Our foreheads pressed against each other, but our lips never touch. I held her hands as she held mine.

"You up for a Starbucks, Wawa, something like that?" I looked up at her and smiled.

"Of course." I smiled as I got up out of bed. She stood around for a moment awkwardly.

"I'll be in the car." I nodded. Minutes later I was on my way downstairs when I was stopped by a little pest.

"Where is it?" I looked down at my sister.

"Where is what exactly?" She crossed her arms and looked up at me.

"You know!" I chuckled.

"Rachel I don't have time for this." I turned around and began to walk away.

"Where are you going!" As I kept walking I shouted back.

"You were adopted!" then my mom jumped in from the other room.

"No, you weren't!" My mother shouted back directing it towards me as she gave me a death stare. I opened the door and walked out. I walked to the car opened the door and sat down.

"It's a bit chilly out huh?" Kylynn asked me.

"Yeah no shit," I said chuckling. She looked at me and smiled.

"Where's your coat?" She asked and I laughed.

"You sound like my mom."

As we traveled down the road I looked out at the street lights. No matter what time of day it was I was scared. It was the inner city and I'm some white kid. It's kind of freaky. Yet tonight I felt safe. Kylynn, she made me feel safe in the harshest of times. I never knew how much someone could make you feel. For the past five months, all she has done was bring me happiness. I could not ask for anyone more special. She made me feel, wanted, and accepted for who I am flaws and all. There was nothing she could do that would get me down. As I looked at her in the car, she seemed like a beacon of hope and love. Yet no one is perfect, and I accepted that. She was mysterious in a way that drew me in closer as if a magnet of love. Though was I just a pawn in her little game, or the king of the kingdom? That I did not know, but all I knew was that she understands me, flaws and all. All that matters is love.

I got home late that night.

"I love you." I leaned in and kissed her. She looked at me afterwards and nodded.

"I know you do." She said softly, I kissed her again and got out of the car. I walked inside the house, it was quiet and the lights were off. I walked up the stairs, each step creaked louder and louder. As I reached my room I shut the door far enough to leave just a crack. I had been getting something from my dresser across the room when my door was pushed open. My father stood in my doorway leaned against the frame of the door.

"When did you get home?" He asked me.

"Not too long ago" I responded, I expected a lecture maybe even something a little harsher. He just remained quiet and nodded. He walked in and looked around at the posters across my room. The Strokes, The Beatles, Arctic Monkeys, The Police, The Arcs, City and Colour, Green Day, and Bowie posters spread all across the walls of my surprisingly small box of a room. He stood away from me looking up at a poster of John Lennon sat behind a large piano. He turned his head in my direction.

"Did you know Bob Dylan introduced the Beatles to weed?" He asked me, that was probably the last thing I ever thought would come out of his mouth. Before I could even open my mouth he spoke again.

"Do you know the Dylan song Positively 4th Street?" I sat in silence, "I thought so, you should listen to it sometime, what do you think it is about?"

"The song?" I asked.

"Yes, the song." He responded with haste. Thanks to my sarcasm and love of breaking his balls I said exactly what he didn't wanna hear, a complete bullshit answer.

"If I had to guess, it is a street that happens to be positive?" He took a deep breath.

"This is why you won't get anywhere, no conviction, no pride in the littlest shit." He began to raise his voice, he stopped himself however due to remembering how late it actually was.

"Look, the song on the surface sounds happy and shit, but just like life it is just gonna show you that there are mountains of shit piled miles high, and you are just gonna have to tunnel through them and deal with it." I put my head down and stayed quiet. He moved from my poster to right in front of me and bent down. His face was inches from me.

"You can't get comfortable in life because you are just gonna lose that shit, you hear me?" He hit me lightly on the side of the head "You will have to learn sometime because right now you are to damn naive to see those mountains of shit right in front of you." He got to the door frame and turned.

"It's gonna fucking bite you in the ass one of these days." He slammed the door. Is it bad to think that was one of our

best father-son moments?

Chapter 6

Two months have passed. To this day I am not sure why, but she had broken up with me.

It was a hard thing to deal with. Though I can't blame her, she dumped my sorry ass for some very good reasons. I got attached. By attached I don't mean just texting her a lot and being annoying. It was annoying, always keeping tabs on her, getting jealous. I could not help it; it was the very first real relationship I had.

I sat silently in my room alone. Nothing but the light of a candle flickering. I could hear the wind pounding outside. My hands shook and my heart hurt. My room was plagued with darkness and distress. The only light illuminated from the candle burning on the corner of my desk. In my hand was my phone. It sat there leaving nightmares for me from the early past. We were happy yesterday, gone the next. In my mind, a war of shadows ragged. As the blood spilled in my mind I heard voices; some sang out her name, others cried cursing her. The fire spread, where her demons appeared. It was her that always ruled me, and now destroyed me. She had always kept my thoughts on a leash, kept me in line, but ruining my thoughts, limiting me to the big old world. With that freedom back, I was releasing demons inside myself.

I don't even understand the power of my

own thoughts. As I sat alone, something

changed. I was not the same. She was my

senses, my motivation, and now I'm

paralyzed without her.

Chapter 7

In the last 3 months, nothing has changed. Not enough sleep, too much thinking. As I laid in bed one Saturday afternoon, as I had done every day since the breakup. My father had come in to try to "Lift my spirits".

"Get the hell up, you lazy asshole, high school is half way, you have not committed to a college, and you don't even have a job!" I glanced over at the gray-haired man and scowled at him. Oh, how he looked so old, weak, yet angry.

"How dare you…" I said slowly. I looked at him with the tilt of my head as I lifted myself from my bed.

"What did I offend you? Well, guess what? I don't give a flying shit!" He was furious, yet I remain quite.

"Hey dad, why don't you tell your boss to give you a raise, so you can get your family out of debt." I slowly stood up, "Maybe you should do something about your family's future and not come in here and lecture me, I'll be gone within a few more months and there is no way I'm coming back." My dad was pissed.

"What did you say, you no good piece of shit?" Now I was standing up face to face with my father. We looked into each other's eyes, It was like looking into the mirror.

"You want to know what I said?" I questioned him.

"Yeah, I would." He was ready to beat the shit out of me.

"I said…" I waited a moment for dramatic effect, "Fuck you." My father took a step back and nodded.

"Okay…" Then in a matter of seconds, I had a bloody nose and was knocked on my ass.

"Don't ever tell your old man to fuck off." I looked up at him holding my nose.

"Now go find a job, or get the fuck out." He walked out of the room then stopped. "I still love you, but you need to get your fucking act together." He muttered. Then he was gone.

Chapter 8

After my father's and I's fall out, I started to question life. Simple questions: Why am I here? How did I get here? Why does life always seem like a pile of shit? When will I leave this crappy place? All questions that showed signs of progressing slowly to a not so happy place. I knew what I was thinking about. I knew how bad it was. I did not care. I only wanted to be happy, but I found redemption in the strangest way.

One day after school I was walking home and hating life when three cop cars speed past me faster than light.

56

"Maybe I could jump in front of one of them?" Lucky for me I was smart enough. One more car sped past this time an ambulance. I kept on going not thinking about it until I reached my street. I saw the flashing lights down the road, near my house. I started to get nervous. I picked up the pace. As I grew closer and closer I ran faster and faster. Then I saw what I was praying not to see. My house surrounded in police tape, and the ambulance open wheeling three bodies covered in a white sheet. Into the ambulance. A single tear dropped down my ghost white face. My eyes started to water more, and more. Then little by little I allowed myself to cry. I dropped to my knees and began to ball my eyes out.

It was worse than the breakup, worse than anything I ever felt before. The police tried to comfort me while my aunt from California was on her way to bring me home with her to live. She was my only living guardian left that we knew of. The police told me that my family was home waiting for me to arrive when some drunk asshole decided it would be funny to go in and rob my house with his buddies, sadly my family was there and soon they will be 6 feet underground.

The cop then handed me a letter.

"Your father had this in his jacket pocket." He had a look of sorrow on his face as I ripped it from his hands. I looked at the front.

"To Finn: open on your 18th birthday" My birthday was tomorrow. The card was rather simple, not much to it. Inside the letter was two plane tickets. One from Philly to Barcelona, and one from Rome to Philly. The letter had no true context as to why there were plane tickets. All it said was that I would understand it all in time. The message was vague, not much help that my father was now gone and could not explain it to me.

"Thank you. May I go in the house?" At this point, I was able to get my shit together for at least a brief second. The officer looked at his colleagues.

"Uh...sure but only for a little." I nodded and went to the old house. I still to this day don't understand why he let me go. It makes no sense. Yet, I still went to the door I put my hand on the cold door handle. I twisted the knob and entered. I put one foot in the home, I never felt more like a stranger. This house was where I lived, where I grew up, every childhood memory.

Every dollar under my pillow, and present under the tree. The tide of memories flowed throughout my brain. I wanted to go in fast

not because it was my house, but because I

was scared because it was something I

needed to see. I closed my eyes and put my

first foot in the old house then the other. I let

out a breath and opened my eyes. I saw the

stains of blood on the freshly cleaned carpet

my mother begged us not to get dirty.

Policemen walked through the rooms

glancing around and collecting fingerprints.

I quickly looked away from the pool of red

sadness and made my way towards the steps

of the house. I moved slowly up the steps,

my hand slightly touching the wooden

banister, my fingers sliding almost as if

dancing along the stage. As I reached the top

an officer was making his way out of the
bathroom.

"I'm sorry kid-o." He continued on
down the steps yet, I did not answer him. I
just powered forward. When I reached my
room I reached for a photo of my mother,
father, and sister. A tear drop fell on the
photo of a distant memory. I fell back onto
my bed. I was not thinking about my family
though. My mind was thinking about
Kylynn, even in the worst of times she was
in my head. I laid back remembering every
kiss, every hug, every I love you, it's funny
each time I said I love you I meant it even
more. The last time I told her I love you was

the day we broke up. I can't tell you how much I meant it.

My mindset quickly changed though. I wanted to be with my family, I wanted to be anywhere but Earth. I got up from my bed. I opened the door and peered out. As I learned that the coast was clear, slowly I went into the bathroom. I went to the closet and grabbed the belt of a bathrobe. I walked to the bathtub, and stepped onto the side of the tub. I made the one part of the belt into a noose and placed it over my head. I placed the other part of the belt over the shower rod. I already felt the tightening of my neck. One pull and my flame extinguished, no coming back. But I did not pull it. I just looked at myself in the mirror staring, thinking, waiting. I saw something in the mirror it was me still, but I was moving and I had something in my hands. My family was around me waving at me as I left. As I flew away. The vision faded and it was back to just me and the belt around my neck.

"Kylynn would never want me to do this. My family would never want me to do this." I unwrapped the belt and stepped down from the tub. I looked at the letter and I packed a bag with clothes, the money from the jar, all the gift cards I could find, phone charger, an adapter, my phone, headphones, and my wallet. I know what I saw in the mirror and I know where I'm going.

Chapter 9

I spent the night at the police station. It was cold and they had no blanket for me, just a hard pillow. I waited for my aunt to arrive, but I'm not going with her.

It's my birthday today. Again alone. You would think I'm used to it.

I remember the burning sensation of the bright sun beating down on my face outside of the police station. A car pulled up with a not so familiar face, the window rolled down.

"Ah, Finn how nice to see you! I'm so sorry love." You could tell she was fighting back tears.

"It's okay." It really was not okay at all, she had not been around for years. I don't even know when the last time I saw her was. I explained to her how I would not be attending the funeral, It was not something I could handle.

"But you have to!" She exclaimed. However, I stuck to my guns. It's not like too many people would even be there.

"No, I will not see them. I wanna go to their graves when it is all done and over with and that's all." She looked at me like I was some freak. Well, I really am though, I did just try to kill myself not long ago.

"Fine, we go when everything is taken care of." I won.

"Oh Finn, where are your bags?" I only had the bag on my back.

"This is all I need." I said, "the rest I want to be donated, or burned I don't really care." Where I'm going, none of that is needed.

For A week or so we had stayed in a shitty hotel until everything was done and over with. It seemed like the time passed so slow. We were on our way to the cemetery.

When my aunt pulled in she did not get out of the car. She was not fond of my parents. So I exited on my own. I walked to the three gray headstones. The walk seemed longer than it should have. It was a dirt path that had graves on both sides. There was a tree that sat right behind the headstones near my family's graves. I watched the tree as it swayed back and forth. It stood alone like a lighthouse on a lonely shore waiting to guide the way for a ship on the rough sea. Am I that ship, traveling with no true purpose? It was beaten and worn down, bark falling off branches hanging by what seemed to be a thread. I knew the way the tree felt, alone and barely alive. It was probably wishing to just be chopped down, wanting to end its life. It has sat alone for years and years. It probably had three friends, all of which had been cut down to make room for the bones of the deceased. There were only two leaves that sat atop the towering tree. Why have they not fallen? The entire tree was dead but the two leaves. Why must they suffer alone? As I approached the graves I looked down on them. I got down on one knee. I wanted to cry, I wanted to scream.

"I'm going to find who I am guys. I'll be back, not sure when, but when you see your son again you will be happy you gave him this opportunity to save himself."

A single tear dripped down my face. I stood up, patted each of the stones, and began to walk away.

"Oh and one more thing." I stopped and looked behind me at the third stone "I hope I was a good big brother."

Chapter 10

When we got to the airport, we went through security and made it to the boarding area. My aunt handed me my passport.

"Don't lose this okay?" She spoke.

"Understood." I walked away and went to the Starbucks in the airport. When I walked back to my aunt she was slumped back head in her knees. She was asleep. This was my chance. I pulled the letter from my father out of my pocket, opened the card inside the card that read:

"To my beloved son," two plane tickets one to Barcelona from Philadelphia and one from Rome to Philadelphia. The plane boards in ten minutes. I began walking prepared for a chance at redemption. When I got to the boarding platform I handed my them the ticket and they handed it back to me. I walked forward through the hallway onto the plane. My seat was a window seat in the back of the plane. I sat down in the row. I just wanted the plane to leave so I would not get caught. Within the next few moments the plane began to move. Then in no time, the plane was off the ground and on its six-hour flight to Barcelona.

There were about two hours left in the flight and I could not sleep. I looked out the window at the curve of the Earth just thinking, thinking about my family, about Kylynn, about who I am. As I zoned out, something caught my eye. On a cloud floating in the sky I saw a white figure standing on the marshmallow like cloud. She tried to say something to me as if relaying a message, a symbol of hope for my broken heart. The cloud got closer and closer. It was a young girl, younger than Kylynn, but the age of my passed sister. The cloud got to the point where I could see it was my sister. She held a long case. As I watched harder the ghostly figure of love started to disappear. As it turned into air it pulled out a necklace I gave to Kylynn before we broke up. For the last moment, I saw the figure let go of the necklace, dropping the golden chain into the ocean. I snapped back to reality.

****

"This is your captain speaking. Fifteen minutes till we land. Begin to shut down electronic items, thank you, and I hope you enjoyed flying with us!" When the plane landed I was scared. I did not know where I was going so I followed the crowd of people to the customs office (at least I think it was the customs office). I handed my passport to the short man who spoke very little English. After a few questions he stamped my passport.

"Welcome to Spain, my new American friend!"

"Yeah, thanks for the help." I walked away and turned to take one last look at the man. He was still smiling as he waved me goodbye. Lucky for me there was a Starbucks in the airport. It was not the best drink I ever had, but it was worth the energy. I went to the ATM and transferred a little bit of my birthday money into euros (Enough to get me to France by train). I exited the airport and flagged down a taxi.

When he pulled up I entered and asked him to take me to the train station. The man spoke little to no English so it took some time and a lot of charades to get him to understand what "Choo, Choo" meant. During the five-minute drive, the extremely positive man tried making conversation with me. I could not understand him in the slightest so I just smiled and nodded hoping for the best. The payment was about ten euro. I said a final goodbye to the cheery man and was on my way.

The train station was very crowded with gypsies, beggars, and just people trying to get to wherever they might be going. I, on the other hand was on a mission to find myself. I bought myself two tickets one to Perpignan, then from there to Arles (both in France). From Arles, I'm not sure what I will do though. I had a notebook with me and I wrote in it each day, talking about the people I met and the experiences I shared.

As I boarded the train I heard the sound of a flute being played. It was beautiful as I got on the train I saw the Flute player draped in all black. As I watched the man play from my seat on the train he let go of the flute when it hit the ground and it disappeared into nothing. The music continued on. The man let down his black hood. I could make out what I thought was my father. He started to walk to the train slowly disappearing like the lady on the cloud. I blinked and he was gone. Then my head began to move to the side. My head stopped when it was looking at the empty seat in front of me. My father's eyes met with mine. He held a letter I wrote to Kylynn on our three-month anniversary then he pulled out a lighter. A large flame shot from it. My father lit the letter on fire. The figure pulled the hood over his head once more and began to turn to air.

"Don't let it pass." The figure said.

I found myself staring into blank

space at the people of the station. The train

started off towards my destination.

Chapter 11

I woke to the sound of a baby crying
and the mother singing a song to the young
child. The soft sound of her voice took me
back to when I was a young child, my
mother would sing me songs to calm me
down when I was scared or sad. I miss those
days. When I was young and did not
understand anything when I could just sleep
and play.

Within the next few hours, we
stopped at many different towns. I talked to
many different people listening to them
hearing their stories. Each one different, yet

amazing in their own ways. On the way to Arles, I met a man. He was around the age of 23. He was from America just like me. Our stories were alike in many ways. He lost his family just as I had and made the choice to travel the world. He was a Native American. At the end of our short ride together he gave me something. It was a Native American flute. He showed me a few notes and gave me the instrument.

"Good luck on your adventure my friend." He told me.

"To you as well." The train pulled into the station as we walked off the train he looked back at me.

"Don't let it pass Finn." I look at him with a tilt of my head.

"Yeah." He turned and looked at me as he walked away. He winked and that was the last I ever saw of the man. I did not even know his name, but I did not tell him my name, so how did he know mine?

There was a board outside the station. It read bus times and the fares. The bus did not go as far as I hoped. I had to take another train. The farthest I could go was Nice. From there my hope is for me to take a boat to Italy. As the train was on the way to Nice I thought not about my parents, but

Kylynn. I wondered if she missed me if she missed us.

I pulled the flute out of my bag I looked it over. I remembered the notes he showed me. I needed money. We had about 10 minutes until we arrive. There were very few people on the train. I pulled a plastic bowl from my bag which I had been eating from. I placed it on the ground of the train. The people did not even notice me. Then I began playing.

They all began to notice me at the point I let out my first note. I replayed the notes in a different order every few second. They looked at me in confusion, but after their blank stares, there were smiles, then clapping. They placed a few Euro coins and Euro notes. Hardly enough to eat dinner. As I got off the train I was placing the flute in my bag. I walked out off the train and as I walked through the streets of Nice I searched for a way to make it to Italy. I walked through the city. It was loud but beautiful. As I made my way to the seaside part of the city I came across a young girl, she was around the age of 9. She was a beggar. I had no money to give her because I needed it for my own food. But what I did was give her a chocolate bar I had in my backpack. For some strange reason, she spoke English with an American accent. It confused me, but I said nothing. After we talked for some time she told me something.

"Do you know me?" She asked. I was puzzled.

"I don't think so, why?"

"You don't know who I am do you?" She paused a tear rolled down her eye. "Big Brother, Don't let it pass." She reached her hand to me then like the other visions, she began to disappear to air. As she left something appeared on the ground. It was a note that Kylynn passed me when I walked by her in the hallway months ago. I opened it up,

"I love you." Then the note turned to air. I stood there with a blank stare wishing I could go back. I simply put my earbuds in and started back on my hunt for some type of boat to take me to Italy.

Chapter 12

It was about ten at night. I had no place to stay. There was a fishing boat that would bring me in about a week on their next trip. I found a spot on the street that I could stay for the night. It was the first time I could sleep this whole trip. I have been in Europe for one day and I have already been to two countries. I set my bag on the ground and pulled out a blanket that was in my bag, then I took off my jacket I had been wearing and put it in a ball and used it as a pillow. As I laid down on the cold street I thought about my family, about Kylynn.

As the night went on I had strange dreams. Flashing lights, loud noises, yelling was all I could hear in my dream. It was strange. It was like I could not even move I just watched like a ghost. It was a long night. As I woke from my sleep It was around four in the morning. My jet lag was hitting me hard. It was still dark out. I packed up my gear and started off in the darkness. Few cars passed me. Six more days. That's all six days. It's not that long. As I walked the streets on the wall of a building there was a ladder that led to a fire escape which went to the roof. There was no one around. I began to climb towards the roof. The ocean breeze got me good. It was nice but scary because I'm high off the ground. I managed to hold on.

As I reached the roof I felt a sense of relief. A sense of happiness. It was the first time I was happy in a long time. I walked to the ledge of the building and sat down. I looked out at the sunrise. It reminded me of Kylynn. Simply beautiful. I sat there for some time thinking. Mostly about life. As I got up from the ground I looked at my backpack. I pulled the flute from it. I looked around on the roof filled with little rocks. I reached for the flute I placed on the ground moments before. I stood up and I played a few notes for a minute. I stopped and looked out at the view of the city. Then I went back to the street.

As I walked down the street I looked for some place I knew. As I searched for some place to get food. I found a Starbucks. I opened the door and walked in there was a line. As I waited I remembered my gift card I had brought with me. I had a $30.00 gift card. It got mailed to me a few days before my birthday from my aunt who I abandoned at the airport. I also had a McDonalds and Visa gift card.

I bought a drink and a breakfast sandwich. I was surprised they accepted the gift card which had American money on it.

Maybe because I was a kid they let it slide. When I received my order it was the best feeling in the world. I ate the sandwich in seconds and the drink within a few minutes. As I left I felt a bit of pride for some reason. I don't know why but I just did.

As I walked down the street I watched as people walked around not caring about anything at all. They were attached to their phones. I did not understand why. How could people be so unsocial? Then I remembered me. How would I sit in my room away from everything? Avoiding my family. I regret it so much, but I can't get those days back. You can't get anything

back.

Chapter 13

On my second day in Nice, as I walked the streets I found a hotel. I had enough to spend two nights. It came with a free breakfast buffet. On my way to the room, I avoided the elevator. I took the stairs all the way to my room on the third floor. As I entered there was a TV, two beds, and a couch. I began to charge my phone and while it charged I went straight for the shower. It was so relaxing, so humbling. I knew what it was like to be poor for a night. It was terrible. What am I saying? For this whole trip, I will be poor. The water hit against my skin and it was so soothing. I spent what seemed like hours just standing there enjoying it. As I exited the shower. I dried off and put on what little clean clothes I had.

That night as I slept, I had a dream. I was 9, as I walked down the hallway something hit the back of my head. It was an eraser cap. Some kid was throwing them at people calling them names. When the eraser hit me I stopped and stood there. I was frozen. why I'm not sure, but I was.

"What the hell are you looking at?" The kid was much older than me. I stood there silent.

"Hey, dip shit did you hear me?" He began to walk towards me.

"I'm talking to you" He grabbed me by the shirt and pushed me into the wall. He reeked of smoke. He was only what looked like to be 12. He began to say things to me. He told me to jump off a bridge, to hang myself, anything that involved physical harm. He threw me to the floor and began to hit me repeatedly. As he did this he cursed at me, spit on me, and laughed at my pain. After minutes of struggling to get him to stop. I gave up. I realized soon that no teacher would be here to help. I just let him do whatever. There was nothing I could do.

When he finally gave up he looked at me and I looked at him. I saw someone walking up behind him.

"Still taking it?" I looked at him and whispered.

"Behind you" I smiled and closed my eyes. As he went in for the final blow.

He was pulled back by a girl younger than both of us. She was new to the school at the time she pushed him forward. He moved away and towards his class. The girl looked at me. I sat up.

"Am I dead?"

"No silly you're still alive." I watched her. Her smile, her eyes, her long dirty blonde hair. She helped me up.

"Don't let it pass." She walked away. As I turned to look at her walk away I noticed stitched into her bag a name.

"Kylynn Ross" It read.

She was long gone. The dream was over I woke from the memory. I sat up in bed. I was breathing heavily and sweating.

Chapter 14

The rest of the week was a blur. I spent most of it wondering Nice playing the flute for as much money I could get. I spent the money to stay in hotel after hotel. On the day I was supposed to go to the docks I met a man. He too was on his way to Italy. He was an American as well.

"I'm sorry I did not even get your name sir." I looked over at him as we walked through the docks.

"The names Todd Davenport." I nodded

"Finn MacKay." I told him.

"Scottish?"

"My dad, yes." A tinge of sorrow expanded along my face.

"It's a strong name, Finn." He reached his hand out for mine. We shook hands.

"So this boat is taking us to Genoa correct?" He stopped and thought for a moment.

"I believe so Mr. MacKay," I nodded

"Please just Finn." He looked at me and smiled,

"Understood."

As we got to the boat we both handed the fishermen 50 euros and walked down into the bottom of the vessel. The men slammed the door shut. We were on our own. We walked to a table with some chairs and we sat down.

"So Finn why exactly are you on this journey?" Todd asked.

"Just traveling." Sort of the truth. "What about you?"

"Well, I'm not too sure, this whole trip is meant for me to find who I am. My oldest son has been gone for some time now, and after other tragedies, I feel it was time to go on a journey." What were the other tragedies?

"If you don't mind me asking how did your son pass?" Todd sat in silence for a moment. It took him some time to say one word.

"Suicide." My mind began racing.

"How long ago if you don't mind me asking?" He sat back in his chair and thought about it for some time.

"Well over 10 years if not more this coming September, how many years exactly is a bit too much math for me."

"Do you know why?" I felt I was going too far but I did not stop asking questions.

"My family lived in New York City, and I still do. My son was 22 years old. Fresh out of college, he was brilliant. He worked in the south tower of the world trade center. It was September 11th, 2001. He worked a few floors above the impact zone. He didn't go to work that day because he was sick. Yet his girlfriend at the time who worked with him on his floor was in the towers. If you get what I'm saying you would understand how traumatizing it was for him. He couldn't live without her and took drugs up to ease his painful thoughts. It made everything worse and he lost his job on top of everything because of his addiction. He was writing me a birthday card when he overdosed. He wrote something along the lines of 'don't' then the pen scribbled out." I was speechless.

"I'm sorry…" My voice trailed.

"For what?" He asked.

"Your loss."

"Don't, you can't change the past kid." I nodded as he spoke.

"Hey, Todd?" I asked.

"Yes?" I paused for a moment before speaking,

"It's been a long day I'm going to go to bed. See you in the morning."

"Night." In the corner away from the table, there was a cot.

Chapter 15

The whole boat ride I sat on the cot in silence. Todd sat at the table in silence as well. Every few minutes you would hear him cough. His coughs were not normal though, they sounded like he was hacking. It sounded like he was coughing up blood, he mentioned something about a past smoking problem the night prior. I ignored it, and I left it alone.

The next morning, we were told that we had one more day on the boat till we land in Genoa. Another day with Todd, another day with his coughing, another day will his sadness. As I rose from the cot Todd was slumped back in his chair mouth open snoring. He never left the table. I went to the cabinet on the other side of the small room under the rotten decks. When I opened the small creaky doors there was some type of black spiky thing in a plastic bag you would find clementine's in. A tag which was attached to the bag was the word "Oursin". What the hell is an oursin? Yet I was very hungry and that's all that was there to eat. As I walked back to the table Todd began to wake from his sleep. As soon as his eyes opened he saw the bag.

"Oursins! give them here!" I tossed him the bag of black spiked food.

"Todd, what the hell are those things?" He looked at me with a grin on his face.

"These my friend are sea urchins!" He handed me one.

"Sea urchins?" He laughed.

"Yes now eat it. Tell me what you think." I took one bite and within a nanosecond, I was coughing almost as bad as Todd was the night before.

"You like it?" Todd said laughing hysterically.

"It tastes like a fish that was covered in shit and then smothered in salt!" Todd laughed even harder.

"We're going to get along just fine Finn." He said with his laughter died down.

"Hey, Todd how old are you?"

"68 why?" I was quiet for a second.

"Just wondering," I said. Todd was a great guy with some great adventures. He spent the rest of the ride talking about his trips. He never once talked of his family though.

The boat landed in the dock.

"Finn, every man has a story or two. If you have one, you lead the story, but if there are two stories in your life, you let life lead your stories." He looked at me as we stood on the dock. "I'm coming with you Finn." I looked at him with the tilt of my head,

"Okay," I responded.

Chapter 16

As we entered the city (much larger than I expected), Todd led me to a train station. As we moved swiftly through the crowds of people rushing to their destinations, I was in another world. Todd was talking to me, but I heard nothing. My feet seemed to move with the cracks on the floor behind Todd. I looked up to the roof. My whole world was moving faster than hyper speed. I felt like a failure. As I scanned the surrounding in the far right corner at the top of the ceiling a golden light was shining. A woman stepped out of the light.

"Here we go again," I told myself under my breath. The woman was visible, but had light shining off of her. She looked at me, our eyes met, then she closed her dark brown eyes that I had missed seeing each day. She never spoke to me, but she led me. Todd turned right I went straight.

"Finn?" I could not hear him. The ghostly figure of gold watched me.

"Finn?" I could hear Todd; his voice was fading away.

The figure came down in front of me. She held up a photo of a family. Their faces had been blurred out, then the figure left and I was back to reality. I felt a hand on my shoulder.

"Finn? Is everything okay?" I was facing a wall. The tiles were chipped and worn down there were names of people carved into almost every tile. I pressed my hand against the wall, and I put my head down. I was breathing heavily.

"I'm good" I turned and looked at his hand still on the wall. He put his arm around me.

"We have to go Finn." He pulled me away from the wall and led me to the trains. We looked at the train schedules up and down.

"How much money do you have, kid?" He looked at me then back at the board.

"few euros." He looked at me again and sighed.

"I have enough." he looked at the times again then at the prices.

"Finn as far as we can get is Milan but it's a hefty fee for both of us." I looked at him then the times posted on the wall.

"If we're going, we have five minutes." He looked at me and he nodded then faster than I could ever anticipate we were running to the tickets. We ran over to the stand. Todd put down the money.

"Two tickets to Milan." The lady put down the tickets Todd snatched them and ran I followed behind him. Clenching onto my backpack we made it to the train and we saw the doors start to close Todd jumped in one of the doors and held it open for me. As soon as I put one foot on the train it was off. Both of us breathing heavily. Todd started to laugh.

"We made it kid." He was smiling.

"Yeah." We walked over to the seats. There was no one in the train. It was just us. We sat down in seats by the window. There was a plug on the table in front of me. I opened my backpack up and unzipped the bag. I took out the adapter plugged it in then I took out my charger and plugged it in. My phone started charging. After I did this I looked up at Todd and he was already asleep. Two more hours I thought to myself.

Chapter 17

As I opened my eyes I saw a lady walking down the train with a cart. It had food and drinks in the cart. As the lady approached me I pulled out my earphones I was in the middle of listing to "Under Control" by The Strokes. Todd was still asleep. When the lady arrived at our table she smiled at me. She handed me a bag of crackers.

"What would you like to drink?" I glanced over at the cart.

"Two Pepsi's please." She handed me two cans of the soda. The bottle was tall and skinny kind of like an energy drink can but smaller. I placed one in front of Todd. She began to walk away.

"When Is Milan?" She turned around.

"About ten minutes' sir." I nodded.

"Grazie." As she was walking away she responded.

"Prego." I turned my music off. My phone fully charged I placed it on airplane mode to save battery life. I unplugged everything placed it in my bag and cracked open the can of soda. From the second the bottle made the crack then sizzle Todd woke up.

"Finn, did you get me one?" I looked at him and smiled.

"Look down." He looked.

"Oh." He started to laugh.

"Five more minutes." He nodded.

"Hey Todd, where are we going to stay?" He thought for a second.

"If I remember correctly there is a hotel across from the train station actually. I'm not sure the quality, but I heard it's pretty cheap."

"Okay, but how long can we stay there for?"

"One day. Not long, I'm not the biggest fan of Milan anyway. I would rather get out of there as fast as I can." I nodded. The train speed into the station. As I walked off the train onto the long path elevated a few feet above the tracks. We walked down passing benches with people sitting and sleeping on them. We walked past beggars, we walked past people at vending machines. As we made our way to the board of times and prices. Todd was not happy.

"Shit, we don't have enough to get to Venice and stay in the hotel." He put his hands over his head kind of the way the runners do after their race.

"Todd let's just go to the hotel and think this out everything will work out." He put his hands down.

"Alright." We walked past the police station, and down the stairs past the McDonald's at the end of the train station and out of the building. We were in the streets. The traffic was very high. We went to the crosswalk and waited. The police officer stopped the traffic and let us and a group of Asian tourists pass. We went from crosswalk to crosswalk doing the same thing. When we made it to the hotel across the way. We were greeted by a man with the name Jesus. He opened the door for us. As we walked through the lobby I noticed a group of Americans were sitting on the couch, one of which was panicking. They had their bags like they were leaving. We went over to the counter there was a lady on the other side arguing with the worker.

"I don't understand why you won't call the police someone stole my purse with passports in it, my credit cards, my phone, and tablet!" My gaze soon turned away from the argument.

"Welcome to the Michelangelo!" She smiled.

"We need a room. I believe it was reserved and already paid for." I looked at him in confusion.

"Okay, what is your name sir?" He thought for a moment.

"Robert Collins." She looked through the computer a second.

"Sir you are not supposed to be here for a few days." He glanced over at me.

"Well, you see I arrived much earlier than I anticipated." She thought for a second.

"But sir I can't just..." Her voice trailed off as he slipped her a small sum of cash and her attitude changed.

"Jesus will be taking you to your room now, it was a pleasure doing business with you." She smiled at me and called the bellhop over. Jesus led us to our room and let us in. Todd smiled and shut the door.

"Todd what did you do?" He started to laugh.

"Okay Finn in the train station at Genoa I overheard this guy saying he was staying here and his name was Robert Collins, so I took the chance for a somewhat free room!" He was still laughing, then I went from a straight face to laughing.

"We're only staying the night Finn then were leaving to Venice okay? I know a good hotel cheap too we can stay there for two days." He was still laughing. He put his hands on my shoulders.

"Let's conquer Italy!" He smiled He looked over at the mini bar

"You know the bellhop told me all the stuff in the mini bar is free right?" I looked over at the mini bar. Todd grabbed the coke. When I got there I grabbed the sprite. There was still food left.

"Finn you put half in your bag and I'll put half in mine." I looked over at the window overlooking the city.

"Finn what are you doing?" I smiled while the glare of the sunset danced across my face.

"Just taking everything in." He grinned at me.

"Sounds good."

Chapter 18

For the first time in what seemed like years, I slept well. Todd may have been loud and coughed in his sleep but I did not mind because I woke up happy and refreshed. As Todd slept in, I wrote him a note telling him I was going down to the buffet so in case he woke up he would know. I walked over to the door and shut it. It locked by itself and I walked down the hall to the back stairwell. I am terrified of elevators so I avoided them as best as I can. I opened door after door traveling down to the ground. When I opened the door to the lobby there were more people coming in (no Robert Collins hopefully) I walked down some stairs to the buffet. I walked through the lines with two plates (One for me one for Todd). I got more than I could ever eat then I got this thing called exotic juice. No idea what it was but damn it was good. I was passed through the lobby to bring the food back to the room, back to Todd, and back to the Wi-F. I walked up the stairs through the hallway to the room. I opened the door and placed the food on the table. Todd was still asleep. I crumpled up the note and threw it at Todd.

"Get up I have breakfast." Todd shot up faster than a gun ever could shoot.

"Food?" I nodded.

"Sounds good to me let's eat and get the hell out of here." I laughed.

"Alright sounds like a plan." Todd ate faster than a racehorse. I ate relatively slow. When he was done he was grabbing as much free stuff in the room as he could because, well it's free. By the time I finished my last bite of food Todd was packed up and ready to go. I stood up took both our plates opened the door and placed them outside the room. I shut the door again, when I looked back Todd had his backpack on and was ready to go. I'm not sure whether he was getting worried about Robert Collins or he was just really tired of Milan. I unplugged my phone put my last bit of stuff in my bag and was off and ready to go. We walked down the stairwell to the lobby. Todd led us through the lobby as he walked by the desk not stopping or looking at the girl behind the desk he dropped the keys on the desk.

We walked out past Jesus he tipped his cap to us as we walked down the street and across the road the sun shining against us. We walked through the crowds of people all yelling in different languages trying to keep in contact with their families who seemed miles apart yet were only two feet away. We walked past the beggars and the mothers holding on to their children. We arrived at the ticket booth. We stood feet away from the ticket booth.

"How much money do you have Finn?" I thought for some time.

"20," I answered. Todd nodded.

"You can get a ticket." He breathed heavily once then coughed.

"How much do you have?" He closed his eyes and took a second before he answered.

"You can get one, but I'll have to figure something out." I put my hands on my head.

"Don't panic Finn this is what is going to happen, you buy your ticket then start

walking to the train I will trail behind. You run into someone and bring them to the ground, don't make it obvious. While you are apologizing and helping them get up I will walk past and grab his wallet. I'll go to the nearest bench get the money I need and then drop it behind them. Stall them until I finish." I looked at him.

"But..." He grabbed me.

"But nothing you have to trust me, now go!" I nodded.

I walked over to the booth got my ticket.

"Hi, one ticket to Venice please?" She waited for it to print. I handed her the money and she gave me the ticket. I glanced over at Todd he nodded at me.

"Grazie." I started to walk towards the victim. I looked back Todd was a few feet behind me. As I got closer to the victim my head was racing then it happened.

"Oh my god I'm so sorry." The man looked frazzled.

"Are you okay sir?" Todd was behind him his hand reaching out for his wallet. "It was my fault I tripped and I'm just so clumsy." We stood up. Todd was already at the bench with the wallet.

"Hey, can you give me directions to the last supper I just got here and I really need to get there?" By the time the words got out of my mouth the wallet was on the ground and Todd was at the booth. While the man was in the middle of his sentence I stopped him.

"Hey is that your wallet on the ground?" The man turned and picked it up.

"Grazie" He walked away not even finishing giving the directions I needed. Todd walked past me fast.

"Two minutes let's go." We raced for the train we got to our section and got on with seconds to spare. We sat down at our seat.

"How did you?" He chuckled.

"When I was young my family was very poor so I got good, I'm not proud of it but it's a great thing to be good at some times." I nodded. The train started off towards our destination. Again within minutes, Todd was sleeping. I watched as the world went speeding by. The first city, the countryside, mountains, and water. It was beautiful. Almost like Kylynn. I went into my phone and searched through my phone until I found a picture of me and Kylynn at a party. We were hugging, we were happy. The photo was taken only days before she broke up with me, out of the blue. She stopped talking to me in those last few days. I would text her but she would never respond. Then on that last day, she responded, and I cried and cried. Not because I was sad but because I loved her. All I wanted was my old life back. That was all. Nothing more. Just my old life back.

Chapter 19

As the ride came to the closing moments. I thought about the journey. About my decisions, about leaving my aunt asleep in the airport slumped back on the pleather chair. I felt bad about some of my choices, but did I? Not really. I never really liked her that much. Eventually, Todd woke from his slumber of snoring and coughing for two hours after eating his feast of pastries and exotic juice he kept in his bag from the hotel.

"How much longer?" Todd was slurring his words and eyes hardly open.

"Ten minutes Todd." He nodded and coughed again. Then within a second, he was out.

"I'll wake you up." I knew he could not hear me, he was asleep.

"Just sleep." I unplugged everything, put it in my bag, and just watched the sea as we entered the city of the water.

The train rolled into the station. We exited the train slower. I feel like over time our bodies have slowed down and are turning to mush. I have never been so tired in my life. I don't remember much of the train station, the memory sort of blurred in my mind. I do remember however, walking

138

out and going down the steps to the water taxis. We went through and retrieved the tickets, getting in the taxi, and making our way to the other side of the grand canal.

"So Todd," Todd looked at me he had sunglasses on.

"So Finn." He smiled and giggled a bit. I smiled back at him.

"Where will we be staying Robert Collins?" I chuckled.

"The hotel Santa Marina." I smiled and Nodded.

"Beautiful name, any clue how to get there?" I questioned.

"Not the slightest." He chuckled again. The taxi landed at the port. We asked for directions to the hotel and the small tan man gave us the general direction, but not much more than that. The city was much more confusing than I expected. There were no roads, but alleys, bridges, and pathways next to the canals. Occasionally you would stumble across a small square with some children playing soccer. The children in one square in particular spray painted a goal on the wall and were taking shots which were all hitting the upper 90 like Pirlo would on a free kick. The children were barefoot playing with a beaten up ball and ripped shirts. The beautiful game was those kids lives. They had no Wi-Fi, no phones, no computer. Just some spray paint and a soccer ball. The funny thing was, they were happy. Poor, but happy. After hours of searching, we came across a rather large square again where children were playing soccer. Todd and I stood in the middle of the rather large square.

"Hello mister," Todd was trying to get in contact with someone. A man around the age of 40 pointed at himself with a "you talking to me?" look.

"Yes you, where's the Hotel Santa Marina?" The man pointed in the direction straight ahead, then started to walk away.

"Grazie." Todd shook his head. He then coughed this time it was not good. Todd looked at his hand after coughing into it. It stopped for a second and looked at his hand. He simply wiped something on his pants and carried on. We walked thru once more another alley and into another square where the large yellow building sat.

"Ah, the Santa Marina!" Todd smiled. As Todd looked up at the building from just outside the ally I broke his spirit.

"We are out of money Todd." He looked at me.

"What about the ten we found on the ground of the train station?" He asked.

"Spent it on the taxi," I spoke as Todd coughed again.

"Well shit." I started to walk past Todd. He stood there just confused about what to do. I walked out to the middle of the square. I took my backpack off and unzipped the bag.

"Finn?" Todd called out to me confused. I walked over to a shop across the way, a sign said "we buy gold" in big letters.

"Finn?" I walked into the shop and placed a gold necklace that had been gifted to me by my mother on my 15th birthday on the counter, it meant a lot to me.

"How much?" I asked the older gentlemen behind the counter.

"Two hundred and change." He said. It was not nearly enough for the hotel.

"How about twenty and you pay for my hotel room?" I bartered, he thought for a moment.

"Alright." He reached out and shook my hand. He took the necklace and handed me the cash for the room. I thanked him and went towards the hotel. I signaled for Todd and walked in the hotel.

"How long are you staying for?" The man at the desk asked. Todd thought for a moment.

"Me and the lad were hoping two nights," Todd said and placed the money down. The man then handed us a key.

"Follow me to your room."

Chapter 20

I got up out of the bed that was close to the floor near the window. I walked up to the window and opened the shutters. A man looked up at me and waved.

"Ciao!" I said, then I shut the shutters.

"Get up." I threw a sock from my bag at Todd. When it hit him he jumped a bit.

"What in the hell do you want?" He coughed.

"We're going to Saint Mark's Square." He sat up and let his feet dangle off the side of the bed that was more elevated than mine.

"Will there be food?" I chuckled.

"If you want food we can get some." He laughed.

"Alright let's go."

As we walked down the stairs and to the lobby we stopped at the desk.

"Now how do we get to Saint Mark's Square?" He thought for a second then handed us a map.

"I circled Saint Mark's Square for you, but just remember the city is much more confusing than the map says." We nodded. We turned and walked out of the building and were on our way.

After about an hour of searching for the square I thought it was about time to talk to Todd about some other things.

"Hey, Todd." He looked at me as we walked from ally to ally.

"Yes?" I thought for a second.

"Did you have any other kids?" He was silent for some time.

"Yes. His name was Tim." I was confused.

"Was?" Todd coughed.

"He died." I put my head down.

"Oh." Todd cleared his throat.

"I already know you are going to ask so I might as well tell you. He died in a car accident when he was 19. His friend was driving drunk." I looked at the canal as we went over a bridge. I quickly changed the subject.

"Hey look we're here!" Todd nodded.

"Yeah, why don't we eat?" I nodded.

"I saw a pizza place just outside the square, I thought it would be good." Todd nodded. He stayed silent for a while when we ate. Something was going on in his head, but I just could not figure it out.

Chapter 21

I got up relatively early that morning. I packed my things and Todd's things like Todd would want I grabbed all the free stuff in the room and went outside to the shop in the square and got two cokes.

"Todd?" I shook him and he coughed.

"What?" I pulled him out of bed and up on his feet. There was blood on his shirt. I said nothing about it and acted like I did not notice it. He walked into the bathroom to change.

"Hey, Finn did you get the free stuff?" He shouted from the bathroom. I shouted back

"Yes, Todd." Within the minute he walked out in a t-shirt and jeans on.

"Looking good." He smiled.

"You changing?" I laughed.

"Do I smell?" He chuckled.

"Not really."

"Then I'm good." He smiled.

"You ever been to Canada Finn?" He asked me

"Honestly I can't say I have," I responded. I was curious to see where he was going with this.

"It was a few years ago, just after my wife passed she wanted me to go out and meet new people after she was gone. She didn't want me to be a hobbit." He told me

"A fair point," I responded.

"So she passed and 6 or so months later I tried internet dating, I know a bad idea. So I was talking to this girl from Canada here name was Kayla or something along those lines, actually, it was a name very similar to my wife's but that's not important." I didn't plan on stopping him "So this girl Kayla was getting kind of flirty and what not, we would talk on the phone here and there but it was mostly texting, I would have video chatted or whatever you kids call it but I am not so good with technology and all that jazz. I wanted to send her a birthday present so she gave me her address. She gave it to me, and because I am the classiest gentleman you have ever met I decided I'd travel to see her myself. Now when I say this girl lived in the middle of nowhere I mean nowhere.

154

So I bought a plane ticket to some little shithole airport in the fucking tundra, not only that but I had to rent some even shittier car with heating that worked maybe 40% of the time and drive another 100 miles deeper into the snow. Now at this point, I am ready to move this girl back to NYC because there was no chance in hell I'd do this again. So I arrived at her little shack, no other houses in sight for miles. So I knock on the door and this 6-foot dude answers the door in his skivvies, the guy had enough blubber on his body to hibernate himself through the fucking winter." Todd started

laughing so hard "And then this

fucker proceeds to try and hug me

saying he loved me and shit. I was

nice about the whole thing but holy

hell was I livid. So I gave the lonely

bastard the gift and made my way

back to the airport. When I got back

to the city I shut that account down

and started traveling and meeting

people that way." I was shocked at

how incredible the story was. It was

almost as if it was made up, but it

was so crazy and

unpredictable that it had to be real. Eventually, we walked down the steps and to the lobby. The group that we saw at Milan was talking to the man at the desk.

It took more time than I anticipated, but when we arrived at the station and we bought our tickets. We waited for about an hour until our train arrived. Todd and I sat and talked about what we have dealt with in our lives. After days of living with a man I never talked to in my life till just days ago I felt it was time to talk to Todd about Kylynn and my family. I explained my story. About my relationship (excluding the name), about my dark thoughts, about my family's death, about my aunt, and how I left my aunt on the pleather chair, and the visions of my family. As I finished my story a tear rolled down my face. I wanted to sob, but I did not. Todd knew what it was like to lose someone you loved so unexpectedly. He hugged me and I knew the connection we had was strong.

We got on the train sat down, and like normal Todd coughed then fell asleep.

Chapter 22

It was noon. The train rolled into the station in Florence.

"Todd get up." Todd jumped up.

"What?" He rubbed his eyes.

"Let's go, we're here." I threw my bag on my back and walked down and out of the train. As Todd and I walked out of the station we did not talk much. We walked down the street still not talking to me. I decided to break the ice.

"So let's get food and figure everything out okay?" Todd was not acting like himself.

"Whatever." He reached into the inside pocket of his jacket and pulled out a flask.

"Um, Todd?" Was this why he was not himself?

"Sorry, I just need it right now." I nodded

"Okay." He coughed again this time the worst one that I have heard in a while. I changed the topic.

"There's a place to eat right there let's go and figure out what we will be doing."

As we walked towards the restaurant I watched Todd. Usually he was grinning and waving at people as we go along, but today he was in a piss poor mood. He had a blank stare on his face, did not even say thank you to the waiter like he did. As we sat down he coughed extremely hard.

"We're not staying in Florence Finn." I looked at him with the tilt of my head.

"What?" He still had a blank stare on his face.

"It's a tourist trap here, there will be no room open at any hotel here. I heard about this place up in Tuscany it's about an hour away. I think it's called the Medici village or something like that. Plus, we'd spent less money would be spent." I nodded sounds good. Then to my surprise, he smiled.

"Good."

Chapter 23

As we stood on the side of the road cars sped past us. Todd whistled one time really loud, coughed hard, then raised his hand and to his surprise, a taxi noticed the large man waving him down. We opened the back door and got in.

"You know how to get to the Medici Villa up in Tuscany?" Todd said unconvincingly enough.

"Hotel Paggeria Medicea?" Todd looked at me and shrugged.

"Sure that place sounds fine." Todd seemed convinced that it was the right place, although I had my doubts about it.

"One hour." He turned away from looking at us and zoomed away, because I guess it's a custom in Italy to drive extremely fast and scare the shit out of tourists.

"Todd why do you know so much?" He surprisingly was not asleep for the ride.

"So much?" He chuckled coughed and continued on, "I know everything Finn."

"Yeah right." He laughed harder.

"I have a photographic memory Finn, I know everything." I laughed.

"Whatever." His grin didn't leave his face. Amidst the laughter I looked up at the meter that told the time left and the cost.

"Ten minutes Todd." He nodded. Time past slow. We traveled up a long windy road that lead to the village. As we went up the hill at what seemed a 90 degree angle I looked out at the rolling hills of Tuscany. The blue skies with the combination of the white marshmallow clouds. It was all so beautiful, a true work of God.

Soon the taxi reached the top from which we drove down a long dirt road at the top of the mountain that looked out at the other hills. We pulled up at an old clock tower that marked the entrance of the village. I handed the driver the fee and exited. We were greeted by two men who would take us to where we would purchase our room. They showed us the leather shop, and the gelato shop. They eventually took us to our room, they left us alone for some time. Todd and I talked for some time about his travels. Then I made my way to the bathroom. The moment I would step out of the bathroom would change everything. As I peeked my head out to ask Todd a question I saw Todd collapsing on the floor. I sprinted out to grab him but his body already collapsed to the floor. His body started twisting and turning violently. Todd was undoubtedly having a seizure.

"Todd! Todd!" I screamed as his body flailed. I rushed out of my room out to the courtyard screaming for help,

"Help! He's having a seizure, someone please help!" I shouted to no prevail. I was knocking on the doors that had been in close proximity. People began rushing out of their rooms to see what was the matter.

"He's having a seizure please help!"
A group of 4 or so followed close behind me
into our room. I panicked as I brought them
into the room where Todd was most
certainly dead.

"Here, here he's right here!" I
shouted, but nobody did anything. Not one
individual said a word.

"Son," an older man spoke, "there is
no one here." My eyes looked at him in
disbelief.

"He's right there! You piece of shit
why won't you help?" I turned around to
face the body that laid on the floor, but no

one was there. I had no words to what I had now seen.

"I swear…" My voice trailed off dazed and confused.

"This is a sick joke!" One of the four shouted.

"I'm getting the manager!" another yelled, as they all rushed out of the room.

I stared at the floor where I last saw Todd. Then my emotions turned to anger.

"Where the hell is he!" I yelled. I searched the whole suite. Throwing vases, lamps, and more. I punched mirrors, pulled my hair, and broke anything in sight. "He was right here!" I yelled. I remembered every moment I spent with Todd. I remembered every second.

"Psst, behind you" A voice whispered. "I'm sorry you have to see me like this." He said not looking at me. Todd was lying in the bed. I walked over and sat down at the edge.

"This is it Finn, it's over, I'm ready." He still refused to look at me yet I could only look at him.

"You're all I have left." I said with a voice crack coming close to breaking down,

I grabbed his hand and held on. He coughed again.

"I never told you about my wife did I?" I shook my head.

"After our children passed on my wife was diagnosed with breast cancer. It was diagnosed too late to even attempt to fix it. Chemo didn't help, it only made matters worse. In her last days when I looked at my wife I did not see my wife. I saw someone who was suffering and I could not do anything about it." Todd closed his eyes for a moment and then opened them again and coughed into a napkin that laid on the table next to him. When he put it back I noticed blood on it.

"What was her name?" He closed his eyes again then spoke.

"Her name was Kylynn." I never told Todd Kylynn's name, only about her.

"Oh." I held back from crying. He coughed again this time no blood.

"Can I ask you something Finn?" I looked at him and I gripped his hand tighter.

"Of course." He thought for a moment as if recollecting his thoughts that were racing around his head in his last moments.

"When's your birthday Finn?" I laughed softly, and wiped a tear from my misty eyes.

"June 22." Todd smiled and nodded.

"Now I know everything…" He coughed and chuckled. I smiled back at him still holding on to his hand. We looked at each other for a long time. Then soon his words spoke out soft but to me it sounded like shouting.

"I think I know what my son was trying to tell me Finn." A tear rolled down my face, I quickly wiped it away.

"What did he say Todd?" He looked at me for a moment then responded.

"Don't let It pass." He looked up at me.

"But what does it mean Todd?" He thought for some time. Then for the last time I heard Todd's voice.

"Finn MacKay, it means everything." Todd smiled as he looked at me, and took his last breath. His hand became lifeless, and his eyes shut. His body then faded away. I sat there just holding the air where Todd's hand once was. I soon stood up and I took the blanket he had been under and pulled it over where his head would be. The idea of Todd died peacefully, that's what mattered. Thinking back, he was never really there. I sat in silence. A figure appeared from the back of the room illuminated in gold. She came over and put her arm around me.

"Why me, why me mom, why me?" I began to ball my eyes out shouting why me, why me god why!

"Let it out my son, let it out." She kneeled down and looked into my eyes. "I'm always with you Finn." She hugged me I was crying harder and harder, and every moment brought more pain.

"I miss you." As we hugged she disappeared to air, just like Todd and every other ghost that had visited me, what was next Jiminy Cricket?

Chapter 24

I walked in the bathroom and looked at myself in the mirror. As I watched myself I began to cry uncontrollably. I did not look like myself anymore. I was not myself, who was I even? I am I Todd, or am I me? What even is me? Am I real? Is anything remotely real or is this all a figment of my imagination? There seems to be nothing left and my entire life is melting before my very eyes. At this point I was screaming, crying, shouting. The entire fucking continent could hear me. I was empty and isolated, seemingly no hope of digging myself out of my grave. It's not like I am any different, everyone else I love is 6 feet under and now the idea of Todd is to. In that moment it all hit me, I had nothing left, no more battles, no more hope, no more guilt, and no more anxiety for the situation I have found myself in. It was over, I gave it everything I could. I walked out of the bathroom and laid down in the middle of the room. After a few minutes there was a knock at the door.

"Come on in." I yelled chuckling, I was losing my mind. The man looked around at everything I had broken. He walked in front of me and stood looking down at me.

"And how are you this fine evening?" I asked the man then laughed.

"I am not sure what has occurred but I need you to leave at once." The man stated in broken English.

"Give me the night." I demanded, I quickly rose and was face to face with the man. This reminded me of when me and pops would duke it out. We stared at each other for some time.

"Fine," he said "You leave first thing tomorrow." He began to leave and I stopped him.

"I have to get to Rome." I said. The man stopped at the door and turned his head.

"A group of tourists leave for Rome tomorrow, I'll let the driver know you will be with them." I thanked him and he was gone. That business deal reminded me of Todd, it makes sense though. I am Todd.

Chapter 25

I slept none that night. I laid in bed. I wept through the night. Todd was the one keeping me together on the trip. My family, now Todd. What else does God want to take from me that I love? All I had left was the clothes on my back, and a phone that only works 60% of the time. Around sunrise I got out of bed and went out on the balcony. I leaned against the railing and looked out at the rolling hills. Soon the sun came up and peeked over the hills.

I looked out at the view of the farmland on the hills I noticed things most

181

would pass over at first glance. The sheep and the cattle that walked freely on their land was a beautiful thing. As well as the homes that lay next to the small patches of plowed land on the large hills. I looked over behind the building I was staying at and I could see the people I would be traveling with start to leave their rooms. They had bags with them. This was my time. I moved to my room grabbed the keys and my bag threw everything in my bag and was on my way out the back door. I walked out and through a walkway that led me out in front of where I had been staying. A girl and her family walked down the steps of the room above mine. She had long blond hair and blue eyes. She was the complete opposite of Kylynn, I smiled at her.

"Hey!" She said in a friendly tone. I Just smiled and looked away. I felt something there, something special, but not the love I remembered with Kylynn. I made my way through the canopy like building that separated the village with shops. I opened the door and made my way down. I walked down the hill past the leather shop, past the gelato shop, and outside from underneath the clock tower. I walked down to the bus and stepped up there was a skinny man on board who greeted me.

"Hello! You must be Finn" I nodded.

"I suppose," I said, who even is me?

"There's a seat in the back of the bus, and let's get the show on the road." He put on some aviator sunglasses and sat down next to the bus driver. I made my way to the back of the bus. There was a window seat in the last row. No one sat next to me. The girl sat down on the other side one seat ahead. I kind of just looked at her for a while. She occasionally looked back and smiled hoping I would find the balls to talk to her. Soon the bus started to move down the mountain on its strange almost 90-degree angle road. Soon after long we were down the mountain and on our way to Rome. There was a tray table in front of me. I placed my bag next to me and pulled down the tray table and placed a coke and granola bar I took from the hotel room. I looked back over at the no name girl. She was talking to another girl who had brown hair and was wearing jeans with sandals. I overheard the sandals girl.

"Who's the hippie?" She shrugged her shoulders in a I don't know fashion, and looked back at me and smiled. I looked away from the no name girl and opened my coke and took a sip. I looked out the window at the countryside of Tuscany that was moving ever so fast. I knew everyone was questioning who I was, but that's okay I'm far more than a dirty hipster backpacking Europe; I'm me I think, and that's okay.

I looked back at the girl. She was still talking to sandals girl. I looked away again and laid back in my seat and closed my eyes.

Chapter 26

"Is this thing on?" My eyes shot open. The skinny tour manager was tapping the microphone.

"Well I would like to let everyone know we are entering Rome!" The skinny guy continued talking about the history of Rome but I zoned out and went back to sleep. Soon enough the bus stopped at the Hotel Cardinal Saint Peter. It was kind of modern. I don't plan staying here though, I'm going home. As we got off the bus the skinny man stopped me.

"We called you a taxi, and you will be on your way." I nodded.

"Thank you, I didn't catch your name."

"Evan." I nodded, he handed me a decent amount of cash to survive a day or two in the city.

"Thank you Evan." The taxi pulled in and I looked back at the no name girl. She looked at me and smiled. She is not the one, but she helped me realize something great. I opened the door and got in. She may have been the one who got away, but the memory of some girl I never even talked to stayed with me. I got into the taxi.

"The coliseum please." He pulled away. I looked out at the relatively suburban city. I looked at the beggars and the businessmen walking along the roads. Over time of traveling through the city we came close to the coliseum. When we arrived I paid the 30-euro fee and got out. It was relatively late in the day so there was no one there. I got in and out fast. I moved quickly to the entrance where I paid my entry fee and walked through the inside of the stadium. I walked past security, they nodded to me as I walked up the steps to the first layer of the colosseum. As I looked out at the ancient structure I thought of my trip and the things I have done. I went up another set of stairs. They were very steep. As I walked out on the next layer I looked out and remembered everything that has happened. From Kylynn, to my family, to Todd, even to the no name girl. As I sat at the top of the coliseum and looked out, the figures that guided me lined the horizon, Todd included. The sun was just setting under them. They waved to me and disappeared.

I walked back down the ancient stadium and flagged down a taxi.

The taxi took me to the airport and I paid the 20-euro fee and walked in. I walked past the statue of Leonardo Da Vinci's Vitruvian man, and over to my line, and showed them my ticket and passport. It took 20 minutes to get to the booth. When I got there I handed my stuff and they sent me to security on the other side of the room where they checked me. The closest flight was in 3 hours so after searching for about 30 minutes for my boarding area, I past several booths selling soccer balls, and cigarette packs that said in bold words "Smoking Kills". When I arrived I sat there just waiting and thinking. Eventually, the plane boarded and I was on my way back home, but what even is home at this point.

Chapter 27

As I sat back in my chair with a TV placed in the seat in front of me. I flipped through the movies and came across something interesting. I found a Ben Stiller movie by the name of The Secret Life of Walter Mitty. As I watched it I became inspired. His adventure reminded me of my journey. He searched the world all because a girl inspired him. It was beautiful, but what topped it off was that as I watched and listened to the movie I heard a song quite familiar. I just remember sitting in my seat watching then hearing something. To my surprise I heard the words I never wished to hear again. "Don't Let It Pass" it was a song. Those words came directly from a song that just so happened to be in this movie that is surprisingly alike my own life. I laid back and smiled. It could not have been any better.

As I looked out at the curve that I had seen once before I saw land come into view. As more land came into view we were told our descent was upon us. I closed my eyes and breathed in and out a few times. I was nervous. Would I come back to people cheering and clapping, or would I come back to an angry aunt and airport security?

Soon to my surprise the plane began to land. As we arrived in Philadelphia I closed my eyes breathed in once and let it all out. I stood up and shimmied out of the window seat and walked down the aisle to the door where the plane connected to the airport. As I walked through the plastic tube I placed my hand on the wall and my fingers danced across the wall as I walked. The wall felt like the wallpaper in a hotel hallway. As I exited I found my aunt asleep on the pleather chairs, no security, no nothing but people trying to get to their destination. As I walked through to the exit someone caught my eye. I stopped and just looked at the girl.

"Kylynn?" I stood there in disbelief as she came running to me. She came and jumped into my arms and hugged my long and hard.

"Finn, I... I miss you." I looked at her in shock. "What?" I gently pushed her off of me and put my hands on her shoulders. I was in shock.

"Yeah I, I want you back is there something wrong?" I looked at her and put my hands on her face gently and kissed her forehead. Then I looked at her and shook my head.

"I have been hurt to many times before and It's not happening again, I thought I loved you, but I don't." She backed up and looked at me almost in disbelief.

"But," I shushed her and began to walk away then I stopped and looked back and said my final words to her.

"You're not for me Kylynn, and I went through a lot of shit to learn that". I then smiled at her and turned away and kept on walking.

As I walked out I flagged down a taxi. I had very little American money but enough to get where I needed. As I sat in the back of the taxi I looked through my stuff. My flute, my wallet, my train tickets, my journal that I never wrote in and most special the memory of Todd.

The taxi pulled up to the yard. I paid the driver and got out. I opened the old gate and walked through. Out in the distance, four figures stood tall. As I grew closer I could make out who they were. Ed MacKay, Janet MacKay, Rachel MacKay, and Todd Davenport. As I stood in front of the figures and headstones I smiled. As I looked at them I knew I was safe and sound.

"I'm back."

ACKNOWLEDGEMENTS

Thanks to every man, woman and dog that helped me bring this idea to life. I don't fully understand why you supported me, however I thank you more than you can fully understand.

I'd like to thank these good folks individually,

Family, I know this was new to you but I appreciate the support and trying to figure how in the hell I turned out to enjoy writing and such, thank you for keeping on me to not stop working on the book. Even after I finished it you kept on me to keep writing new things.

Mrs. Healy, thank you for being the first to believe in me. You are a prolific teacher, person, and friend.

Saralynn and Kristy, I truly appreciate you guys taking the time to go through and make this idea the best it could possibly be, it would not be the same without you two.

Italy, my trip to Italy in 2014 heavily influenced the travel within the book, so thank you to the entire country of Italy. You are beautiful people.

And thanks to whoever managed to find the time to read this book, I'm not sure why you did it, but thank you.

About the Author

Alex Pavljuk is an American teenager born December 4th 2001. With the passion for writing, he began his first novel "The Tide" in 2014 and finished in mid 2017. Alex's passions besides writing includes, listening to music and making movies. He often uses his talents of film and photography to capture moments of his life. He plans to continue his journey of creating and publish more of his works in the future.